To McPatti,

Best Wishes,

The Annoying Ghost Kid

Robert Wilson

ROBERT EVANS WILSON, JR.

ISBN:0615576877
ISBN-13:9780615576879

For Evan and Andy,

who asked me to tell them a funny ghost story.

CONTENTS

ACKNOWLEDGMENTS

I would like to thank several people for their inspiration, advice and help. My first thank you goes to my sons Evan and Andy. The inspiration for this book began when they asked me to tell them a ghost story one night at bedtime. I asked what type of ghost story they wanted, and they replied that they wanted a scary one. Ninety seconds into the story, they asked me to stop because I was really scaring them. I then asked them what type of story they wanted instead, and they replied that they wanted a funny ghost story. It was then that I began to create *The Annoying Ghost Kid.* They liked it so much they asked me to tell it again and again, night after night. Then they started telling their friends about it, who also wanted to hear it. Before long, every time I went to visit them at school, kids would ask me to tell the ghost kid story. This went on for years; meanwhile, the story continued to grow. One night, on a Cub Scout camping trip, thirty boys sitting around a campfire started chanting, "Ghost Kid! Ghost Kid!" I knew then it was time to write it down.

My next thank you goes to Evan and Andy's teacher, Kathy Masterton, for allowing me, when I was helping out at the school, to indulge her students with a Ghost Kid story every time they asked to hear one. From her fourth grade class, I'd like to thank the following students for being the first to read the book, and for their positive feedback: Madeline Miller, Annie Moeller, Monica Schweizer, and Michael Toner.

My appreciation also to Debra Selinger for editorial advice. Finally, a special thank you to Previn Hudetz for designing the cover.

1 DISAPPEARING ACT

I was just about to bring down the evil alien warlord's mother ship when, all of a sudden, I heard the most dreaded words any kid could hear.

"Corky, you've played enough video games for today."

"Aw, Mom, I'm just about to destroy the enemy."

"No, that's enough for one day."

"But there's nothing else to do."

"You can go outside and play; a little fresh air will do you good. You've been cooped up in this house for days."

"But, Mom, there's no one to play with."

"There are plenty of kids around here."

"I don't know any of them."

Mom sat down next to me and mussed my hair. "I know you've been lonely since Gary moved away, but you'll make new friends."

"I'll never make another friend like him."

"Yes you will; you just have to get out there and look."

"Where?"

"Go down to the park, I'll bet there are lots of boys on the playground."

"Mom, that's a baby playground. There won't be any kids my age."

"You don't know that until you get there. Now get up and go look for your new best friend."

"But, what do I say if I find someone."

"Just go up and join in whatever they are doing, and the conversation will come naturally."

"OK." I said, but I was not convinced.

When I got close enough to see the park, I recalled my grandfather telling me that it used to be a zoo. He said it had to be closed because some dumb kid was annoying the gorillas by throwing rocks at them. My grandfather wasn't there at the time, but he'd heard about the kid.

I remember him saying, "Corky, that boy had a great throwing arm. His father loved to boast that he'd make a great baseball pitcher one day. But, instead of throwing strikes to batters, he threw rocks at animals.

There wasn't a dog in the neighborhood that would come near him. And, when he went to the zoo, he threw rocks at the gorillas and hit them in the head. Then he would laugh and laugh."

"Didn't anyone try to stop him," I asked.

"Oh, he was a cunning boy, he wouldn't throw rocks when any adults or zoo workers were around. And, if any of the children were to tell on him, he would scream and cry and call them liars."

"And, they believed him."

"Yes. Then one day he hit the biggest gorilla so many times, that it broke out of the cage and got him."

"Got him?" I asked.

"Uh, hmm!" He nodded gravely.

"Oh."

"That's right, no more little trouble maker annoying the gorillas, but then there was a big fuss around town about the zoo being a dangerous place, so they sold all the animals, tore down the cages and made it into playground."

When I reached the park entrance, I stopped and looked at the playground which I had pretty much outgrown. I thought how cool it would be to have a zoo so close to home, if only some annoying kid hadn't ruined it for everyone. I said out loud, "What a loser!"

When I turned to continue walking there was a kid standing right in front of me. I didn't even hear him come up. And, he was crying.

"Hey, what's wrong?" I asked.

"I want my Mommy." He cried.

"Are you lost?"

He just cried, "I want my MOMMY."

"We'll find her. What is your name?"

He cried louder, "I want My MOMMY."

"O.K., O.K." I said, "We'll look for her right now. What does she look like?"

Once again, and even louder, he cried, "I Want My MOMMY."

I looked around but there were no adults in sight. So, I asked him, "Do you live near here?"

All he did was scream, "I WANT MY MOMMEEEE!"

"Okay, Okay!" I yelled.

He might be upset, but he was beginning to get on my nerves. So, not knowing what else to do, I grabbed the boy's hand, walked across the street to the nearest house and rang the doorbell.

A lady opened the door .

"Excuse me, Ma'am," I asked, pointing beside me. "Do you know where this boy lives?"

"What boy?" She asked.

"Why this boy," I said while turning to look behind me. "Huh, where'd he go?" The boy was gone. I looked all around, behind the bushes, around the side of the house, but he was no where to be seen.

I called out, "Little boy, little boy. Where are you?" But no one answered.

The woman looked at me suspiciously and said, "You aren't playing games with me are you?"

I said, "Oh no, ma'm." There really is a boy here. He has light brown curly hair and green eyes. He's wearing a white button up shirt and long blue shorts. He's lost and crying for his mommy.

"Uh huh. That prank's been played on me before young man."

"Prank!" I cried. "I'm not playing a prank. There really is a kid."

She replied sternly, "Well, if you ring my doorbell again. I will call the police."

I wondered why she was being so harsh, but I said, "Sorry, ma'am. I won't ring it, I promise."

She slammed the door and I walked back to the sidewalk. When I got there, the kid was standing on the sidewalk; waiting.

"Hey, kid. Where'd you go?"

"I Want My Mommy!" He yelled.

Oh boy, was this kid annoying. I just wanted to get rid of him. I started to turn back to the lady's house, but then thought better of it, and went to the house next door instead.

A man answered that door and I said, "Hi mister. Do you know this boy or where he lives?"

"What boy?"

"Oh no, not again!" I cried as I swung around. He was gone again. I looked sheepishly back at the man, and said, "He's a lost boy who keeps crying for his mommy."

Just then a phone rang and the man went inside to answer it. While he was gone I started looking for the boy behind the bushes. As far as I could tell it was the only place he had time to hide. But, I couldn't find him anywhere. By the time I finished searching the shrubbery the man came back outside and now he was mad.

"So, this is your idea of a joke; ringing every doorbell on the block. My neighbor next door just phoned to warn me about you. And, I just called the police. Now get out of here!

"I'm sorry, but it's not a joke. I really did..."

The door slammed shut.

"Boy, the people in this neighborhood sure are mean," I thought.

When I got back to the sidewalk, guess who was there? Yeah, the kid.

"What's the idea taking off like that? You made those people think I was playing a prank."

The kid started laughing, "Hee ha, hee ha."

"Hey, it's not funny!" I said. But, he just kept on laughing. "Stop it!" I said, "Or, I'm not going to help you find your mommy."

Then I heard a "Whoop-whoop" sound behind me. I turned around and a police car with its flashing lights on was pulling up next to me.

2 OUCH ACORNS HURT

The cop leaned out his window and asked, "You the boy who thinks it's funny to ring doorbells?"

"Uh, no, sir. I wasn't trying to be funny. I was looking for..." But, before I continued, I looked around for the kid. Just like before, he was gone.

"Looking for what!" The officer demanded.

"Uh, nothing sir." I muttered.

"What's your name, boy?"

"Corky Carson, sir."

"Well, you better move on. If I get another call about you ringing doorbells, I'm going to arrest you."

"Yes, sir." I said, and started walking back home.

Then, just as soon as the police car was out of sight. Someone tapped me on the shoulder. I turned around and it was the kid.

"Hee ha, hee ha!" He laughed.

"AA-YA-YEEEE!" I screamed in terror.

The boy was flying. That's right. Hovering right in front of my face. Then he started flying around and around me. At first I was frozen in fear. So, he started poking me with his finger. I ran. He just flew right behind me laughing.

"Ouch!" Something hit me in the head. Then I was hit again. Then again and again. The kid was pelting me with acorns. He never missed, and he could throw very hard. Those things hurt. Even worse, I couldn't get away from him.

"Ow, ow, ow." Every time I cried out, he laughed. I finally got so annoyed, I picked up a stick and swung it at him. But the stick swung right through him like he wasn't even there. I swung at him again. And, again it went right through him. That's when I got really frightened. I started shaking and the kid laughed even louder.

"What are you?" I shrieked.

That made him laugh so hard he forgot he was flying and crashed right into the sidewalk. His head went below the concrete and his rear-end was sticking up in the air. Suddenly I forgot my fear. It looked so funny, I laughed.

"Now that's an irresistible target!" I said aloud. Then I aimed my foot for his rump and kicked as hard as I could. But, my foot went right through him, and with no resistance to slow down my foot, I fell backwards and landed on my own backside. I could hear him laughing under the sidewalk. I leaped up screaming and ran full force toward home.

He stayed close behind pelting me over and over again with acorns. I saw the broken windows and sagging shutters of the old haunted house up ahead. That meant I was nearly home. As I ran past the creepy, three-story house, I hoped the ghost kid would disappear inside it and leave me alone. He didn't. I could now see my house and safety. Oh, No! Suddenly, I realized that if he knew where I lived he would follow me inside and annoy me for the rest of my life. So, I turned and ran into the woods. I felt an acorn whiz by my head. I zig-zagged to dodge him, but I was getting tired. Pretty soon, I was going to have to stop.

I tried hiding behind a tree, but he flew right through it. I hid behind another tree and he flew through it too. I dodged behind one tree after another hoping he wouldn't see me, but all the trees were too skinny and he could see me. Then I spotted a big old tree that had a huge gnarled trunk. I ran toward that tree at full speed and ducked behind it. I sat there breathing hard. Several long seconds passed and no kid. So, I peered around the edge. Big mistake; he saw me. He came flying toward that tree. But, I was now too tired to run. He kept coming, faster and faster. Then BAM! He crashed into the tree. He didn't pass through it. He slammed into the bark head first. Then he crashed to the ground.

I ran over to him. He wasn't moving. "Oh no!" I said aloud. "Is he dead?"

"Of course, he's dead." A deep, raspy, nasally voice said behind me. "He's a ghost."

I whirled around to see a tiny, very old man with pointed ears. "Who..., who are you?"

"I'm the elf who lives in this tree." He said in irritation. "I'm the elf that you and your ghost friend woke up. And, I'm the elf who's going to turn you into a mushroom."

"Hey, he's not my friend, he was annoying me and I was trying to get away from him."

"And, so you brought him into my woods?"

This elf was really cranky. So, I said, "No, he chased me here. But, I'm sorry we woke you."

He seemed to accept my apology and started to go back into the hole at the bottom of the tree.

"Hey, wait a minute!" I said. "How come the ghost boy couldn't fly through your tree?"

"That's because I touched it."

"What does that mean?" I asked.

"It means it's enchanted. Anything an elf touches becomes enchanted. Don't you know anything?"

"I guess, not." I answered. "Heck, I didn't even know there was such things as ghosts and elves until today."

He shook his head, turned back again toward his hole and muttered, "Stupid human."

I noticed the ghost kid was beginning to stir. I called to the elf and said, "Please don't go. One more question."

He gave me an exasperated look, but tilted an ear toward me.

"Would you enchant a stick or something for me, so I can swat him with it in case he follows me home."

"No." He said firmly. "I don't enchant things for stupid humans."

"Why not?" I implored, but he ignored me and disappeared into his hole.

The ghost boy started to stir and I was afraid he'd wake up before I got a chance to get away. So, I took off running. All the way home I kept looking over my shoulder, but luckily no ghost boy. When I got inside the house, my cat Joey was there to greet me.

"Hey, Joey!" I said, "Have you ever seen a ghost?"

"Bbrrrt!" he said, then rubbed against my legs.

I'm not sure what that meant, but I was just glad to be home. I sat on the floor and petted him until he was purring as loud as a lawn mower.

The next day while I was walking to school, I worried about running into that annoying ghost kid by the playground again. So, I decided to play it safe and go a different way. I turned down Cemetery Street. It would take ten minutes longer to get to school, and I'd have to go past the creepy old graveyard. It would be worth it, if I never ran into that kid again.

It worked, at least for a couple of days. Then one morning as I walked by the cemetery, I saw an elderly man and woman putting flowers on some graves just over the fence near the sidewalk. I overheard the old lady say to her husband, "and, this little gravestone belongs to my baby brother, the one who was killed by a gorilla."

I stopped cold, and said, "Excuse me, ma'am." She turned around and looked at me over the white picket fence. I asked, "I heard you say your brother was killed by a gorilla, was he in Africa, like, on a safari or something?"

She smiled at me and said, "No, he was just a little boy, younger than you. He was killed by a gorilla in the old zoo."

Then I had to ask the one question I was afraid to ask, "Ma'am, what did your brother look like?"

"He had light brown curly hair and green eyes and a birthmark on his left arm that looked like a toad."

"A toad... really?" I started laughing.

"Yes, really." She smiled back.

"What was your brother like?"

"Oh, he was a mischievous little imp. He was always getting in trouble. Pulling the cat's tail. Burping in church. Throwing rotten eggs to stink up a room. Sticking his leg out to trip people. Oh, and his favorite was writing his name on other people's stuff."

"What was his name?"

"Duke."

"Duke? Like a dog's name?"

"Yes, but back then people didn't give names like that to their dog. Oftentimes, if parents named their first son Rex, the second son would be called Duke."

"So, Duke had an older brother named Rex?"

"Yes, and he was always trying to be just like his big brother. Unfortunately, Rex wasn't interested in playing with Duke because he was younger and could not keep up. And, to make things worse there were no boys his age for Duke to play with. So, when Rex wouldn't play with him, he would get angry and do things to annoy him."

"Really, like what?" I asked.

"Like break one of his toys. Then you'd hear Rex yelling, "Dukey!"

"DUKEY!" I cried out loud. "Rex called him Dukey?"

"Only when he wanted to make him mad. Duke hated to be called that. So, that's what we all called him whenever he was bad... which was fairly often."

"What did your parents do when he was bad?"

"Nothing. Duke was the baby, so they spoiled him rotten. He always got his way. And, if he didn't, he'd throw a tantrum until he did. And, my parents always gave in."

"So, Dukey was a brat?" I said.

"Yes, you could definitely call him a brat."

"Yeah, I think I know him."

"You mean you know someone like him."

"Yeah, I guess. I met this bratty kid over by the playground who was crying and said he wanted his mommy. But, he was only playing a joke on me. And, then later on he started chasing me and throwing acorns at my head."

"Oh my. Oh my," said the old lady. She turned to her husband, "Those stories we heard before must be true. We better get out of here."

She turned back to me and said, "Young man, stay away from that playground." Then she and her husband hurried off to their car.

I looked over the fence at the small gravestone and read the name Duke.

"So, your name is Dukey?" I said out loud, and laughed, "Ha ha ha ha."

Then I picked up a few acorns and pinged them off his gravestone and started chanting in a singsong voice, "DUKEY! DUKEY! DUKEY! Smells like PUKEY! HA HA HA HA!"

Suddenly, I saw a head pop up out of the ground. A head covered in light brown curly hair. The head started turning around toward me. Uh-Oh. It was him! I ran. But it was too late. He saw me.

3 TROUBLE IN SCHOOL

"Hey, who's callin' me, Dukey?" yelled the annoying ghost kid behind me, but I kept running toward the school. If you think you can outrun a ghost - - I can tell you now - - it can't be done!

I was fifty yards from the school door when he slammed into me from behind. My books went flying forward, and I right behind them. My books hit the sidewalk first. I put out my hands to break my fall. I didn't want my palms to scrape across the concrete, so I aimed for my history book instead. Wrong move.

As soon as I hit it, my book started sliding like a banana peel on ice. My feet were straight up in the air as I did a sliding handstand ten feet down the sidewalk. Finally the book ground to a halt, and I was flung forward into a half somersault. I landed skidding on my behind. My history book's cover was a shredded mess. Boy was I going to get in trouble for that. Worse was the seat of my pants, my crash landing ripped a big hole. It was big enough to fit my hand in.

"Hee ha, hee ha!" I heard the ghost kid laughing. He was laughing so hard, he couldn't stand. He was rolling in the grass behind me.

I wanted to go home and change, but just then the bell started ringing. I pulled out my shirt tail and hoped it would cover the embarrassing hole. I scooped up my books and started running for the door. The last thing I heard as I went through the door was that annoying laugh,

"Hee-ha hee-ha hee-ha ha ha ha!" He sounded like a donkey.

I wondered what was in store for me next. It didn't take long to find out.

I entered my classroom quietly and hoped Mr. Russell wouldn't notice I was late. I slipped into my desk, flipped open my notebook and started to work. Behind me Susie poked the rip in my trouser seat with her shoe and whispered, "Nice pants, Corky."

The rest of the morning went quietly, and I was beginning to think I was going to make it through the rest of the day without a problem when Mr. Russell told us to get out our history books.

He immediately saw the condition of mine, walked over, picked it up and said, "What'd you do Carson, use this for first base?"

The class laughed.

"Uh, no. I, uh..."

"That will be two demerits for destroying school property, plus you'll have to pay for a new book." He dropped the book back onto my desk and headed back to the front of the room.

He started calling on us individually; asking questions about last night's lesson. When he got to me, he asked, "Who was the first President of the United States?"

"All right, an easy one," I thought. But, as I opened my mouth to answer, I heard an extremely loud belch from behind me.

"BURRRRPPP!"

The whole class laughed. I swung around in my desk to look at Susie, whose mouth was shut. She shook her head and pointed back at me like I was the one who did it.

"Mr. Carson," roared Mr. Russell. "Are you looking for another demerit?"

"Uh, n-no sir," I stammered, "It wasn't m..."

"BURRRRPPP!" Another belch from right behind me. It was so loud that no one could hear what I was saying. It just looked to everyone like it was me.

Now, every kid in the class was pointing at me and laughing. I looked around and around trying to find the true culprit. Finally, I looked up and floating upside down with his head just above mine was the ghost kid, with an annoying grin on his face.

I pointed up and said, "Mr. Russell, it's not me, it's..."

"BURRRRPPP!"

"That will be enough, Corky!" Mr. Russell ordered. "You go stand out in the hall until you're ready to control your gastric gasses."

The kids roared in laughter at his choice of words. And, I looked up at Dukey who was floating above me, laughing with them. He grinned at me, then pumped his fist and said, "Yeah!"

That's when I realized that I was the only person in the room who could see him. Everybody thought I was the one burping. If no one else could see the kid, then this was a bigger problem than I imagined.

As I opened the door to leave the classroom, the kid got me one more time. He got right behind me and broke wind with a loud, "P-P-P-P-P-P-P-POOOOTTT!"

My classmates screamed in laughter, and somebody called out, "Hey, look Corky just blew a hole in his pants!"

I slapped my hand over the hole in my pants, but the laughter just rose even louder.

Mr. Russell, yelled, "That's two more demerits, Carson!"

I was so embarrassed. Every kid in the room was looking at me and laughing. Then I noticed one who wasn't.

4 ROTTEN EGGS STINK!

Jill, the prettiest girl in the class, wasn't laughing at me. She wasn't looking at me either. She was staring right above me with eyes as wide open as they could be.

I stopped. I wanted to ask her if she could see my tormentor, but Mr. Russell said, "Now, Mr. Carson."

I hurried on out and pulled the door shut behind me. It was a relief to escape all that laughter, but only momentarily as the kid was still floating and snickering in front of me. I took a swat at him only to see my hand pass right through him.

He broke out with his donkey laugh and swirled around my head thumping me with his fingers.

"How is it that he can thump me and even knock me down on the sidewalk, but I can't hit him?" I wondered.

I didn't know what to do. I just had to figure out a way to deal with him. In the meantime, I slumped to the floor, leaned against the wall and covered my face with my hands, and hoped he'd leave me alone for awhile.

Eventually the ghost got bored and left. I knocked on the door and Mr. Russell let me back in.

But when school let out that afternoon, he was waiting for me. I felt something hit me in the back of the head. I swung around and there he was with a handful of acorns. I knew it was useless to run, so I stopped. When he cocked his arm to throw, I got ready. Then when he tossed the next one I dodged it. He grabbed another and threw it even harder, but I dodged that one, too. He threw another and another and each time I got out of the way.

"Hey, this is fun!" I said.

Each time he missed, he got madder.

"Ha, ha, ha, ha!" I started laughing at him.

His face got red, and he started screaming, "No fair. No fair!"

He threw and I dodged, over and over, until finally he ran out of nuts. He started to fly away.

I yelled out, "Hey, where are you going Dukey? You're not giving up are you? It's just getting fun!"

"Don't call me Dukey!" He hollered back.

"Dukey, Dukey..., Dukey wanna pukey!"

Then he flew off screaming, "MOMMEEEE!"

He got me again the next day. I was on my way to class and stopped to get a drink. Billy, the class clown, was drinking from the fountain and I got in line behind him. When he finished, I bent over and pressed the button, but no water came out. Suddenly my legs felt wet and I looked down. The water was spraying out sideways. I let go of the button and jumped back. But I was too late, the water soaked the front of my tan pants. If I'd only worn my navy blue ones, you wouldn't be able to see it. But on tan, it looked just like I peed in my pants. I looked back down at the water fountain and could see a pink glob of gum pushed down into the hole where the water was supposed to come out.

"Hey, not funny, Billy!" I yelled.

Billy turned around and saw my wet pants and immediately started laughing. "What happened to you, couldn't make it to the bathroom?"

"No, you did this. You put gum in the water fountain."

"No, I didn't!" He insisted. Then he came over to look. "I don't even chew pink gum, only sour apple which is green. See." He stuck out his tongue and blew a bubble to prove it.

I remembered that was true, I'd never seen him chew anything but the green stuff. Then I heard laughter from behind me, "Hee ha, hee ha, hee ha ha ha ha!"

I spun around, but there was no one. The braying laughter continued, and I spun around again. And, again nothing. I looked up and down, but couldn't see him.

Billy said, "What are you doing?"

"I'm looking for someone." I said.

Then I noticed Jill walking toward me, her long ponytail swaying back and forth. I'd been mesmerized by that ponytail for years. Now she was heading my way. She stopped right in front of me; her big blue eyes stared over my shoulder.

"You see him don't you?"

She nodded.

"For some reason I can only hear him, today."

"Well, that could be because he's getting ready to throw an egg at you."

"What!" I cried.

"Duck!" She yelled and pulled me down.

I heard a whooshing sound over my head, then the crack and splat of an egg hitting the wall. He missed.

"Pee Yew!" She cried. "That egg is rotten. Gross, now the whole hallway stinks."

"Thanks for saving me."

"You're welcome. Oh, no," Jill cried, "Run!"

"No, if I run, he'll get me. I've got to dodge it. You tell me which way to jump."

"Okay, he's aiming..., get ready... LEFT!"

We both jumped to the left. I felt the egg brush my shirt sleeve, but it kept going and smashed into the floor.

"Whew, that's nasty!" I said as it splashed near us.

"Here's comes another one... DUCK RIGHT!"

He missed again.

Suddenly I saw him appear. He was out of eggs and screaming, "No Fair! No Fair!"

He then noticed Jill, and realized that she could see him too, and he flew over and pulled her long ponytail.

"OUCH!" she cried.

He pulled it again.

"Ow! Make him stop."

I was powerless to help her. I'd have given anything for an enchanted tennis racket at that moment. One swat would've whacked him into the next county. Point-Game-Set-Match!

He yanked her ponytail a third time. Finally inspiration dawned; I took off my jacket and threw it over her head.

"Where'd she go?" He was completely puzzled. I never said he was smart... only annoying.

Then as usual he got mad, and came flying right at me. I ducked and he missed. He tried it again and missed. I was getting pretty good at this. I pretended to be a matador holding out my cape and yelled, "Toro! Toro!" The kid flew at me one more time, and again he missed. Now it was me who was annoying the ghost, so I started laughing. He got upset and flew away.

Just then, the bell rang. Jill and I ran for class. I thought we were rid of him for the day. Boy was I wrong.

5 BEWARE THE MAILBOX

When I got home, I stopped at the mailbox to get the mail. I pulled open the door and out burst the ghost kid shrieking, "BLEEE-ah-EEE-ah-EEE!!!"

I was so startled, I screamed and leapt backward into the street right in front of an oncoming car. The driver slammed on the brakes and the car came to a tire-squealing halt only inches from hitting me.

I was so scared, I couldn't even move. I just stood there shivering. The man in the car blew his horn at me. Then he yelled some words at me that I'm not allowed to repeat. Finally, he backed up his car and drove around me, shaking his fist as he went past.

Meanwhile, the ghost kid was laughing so hard he was rolling on my driveway, "Hee ha, hee ha, hee ha ha ha ha." Boy, did I hate that sound!

I sat on the curb and ignored him. After a while, satisfied that he'd totally ruined my day, donkey boy finally flew off.

The next day though, he did the same thing. I had taken three tests that day in school, so I wasn't thinking about ghosts. Just as I opened the mailbox, he came flying out yelling, "BLEEE-ah-EEE-ah-EEE!!!"

I should have expected it, but he got me again. I yelped, and jumped backwards into the street, but at least this time there weren't any cars coming. Dukey exploded into his braying laugh, and followed me all the way up to my front door. The jerk.

When I went inside, my mother said, "Corky, who is your new friend?"

"He's not my friend."

"Are you sure? He sure looks like a friend to me."

"You can see him!" I spun around and looked back out the door.

"Not now, he must have gone home, but I saw him following you up the walk."

"Well, he's not a friend. He's a pest and he's mean."

"A little guy like that? Surely you exaggerate. He just wants to play with you."

"He's always playing tricks on me; and that's not all he's a gho..." I stopped myself. Mom would never believe me.

"He's just trying to get your attention, so you'll play with him. Give him a chance, it's not like you have a lot of friends."

"Sure, Mom. Can I play video games now."

"OK, but just until dinner."

Duke continued to play the mailbox prank every day without tiring of the joke even though I was no longer frightened by it. The good news was that he was becoming predictable which helped me come up with a plan to get even.

I asked Jill to come over Saturday morning. When she arrived, I noticed she wasn't wearing a ponytail.

"Are you ready to go to the hardware store?" She asked.

"Let's go."

On the way, Jill watched for the ghost kid. She didn't see him anywhere, so we went on into the hardware store where I bought a new mailbox. One that looked just like our old mailbox except this one had a front door and a back door. I also bought an air horn. The biggest one they had and loud enough for a boat lost in the fog. I pushed the button on the back to make sure. "WAAAAAAAAH!"

Jill slapped her hands over her ears and yelled, "Ow!"

Then the store manager yelled at me, "Hey, kid, not in the store!"

Back at home, Jill kept on looking out, while I got my Dad's screwdriver. I took off the old mailbox and replaced it with the new one. Then we went inside and waited for the mail.

When I saw the postman pull up to our mailbox, I opened the front door and then yelled back inside the house, "Mom, the mail is here!"

Jill watched the mailbox. "I don't see him."

So I yelled again, "Mom, the mail is here. Do you want me to go get it?"

My Mom walked into the room, and asked, "What's all the yelling about?"

"Oh, hi Mom. Nothing. Just wanted to know if you wanted me to get the mail."

She looked at me like I was a little crazy, and said, "Sure, go ahead."

So, I yelled out the door, "OK Mom, I'm going to get the mail."

My mom shook her head and walked out of the room.

Then Jill whispered, "I just saw the ghost kid fly into the mailbox."

I put the air horn under my shirt and walked quietly on the grass, so he wouldn't hear me coming. I went to the back of the mailbox and pulled out the air horn. I put my finger on the button, and my other hand on the back door handle. Then I yanked open the door, shoved in the horn and pushed the button, "WAAAAAAAAH!"

The front door blew open and the ghost kid shot out of the end like a screaming cannonball, "AIEEEEEEEE!" He sped toward the big old tree across the street and I figured he was going to pass right through it. But, to my happy surprise he hit it and bounced. It must've been another elf tree because ghost boy ricocheted right back into the street just in time to meet a truck racing by. The kid passed right through the truck, but the current of air created by the truck sent him spinning in an arc toward the car coming from the other direction. *Whoosh*, that car sent him spinning back across the road into another car. Traffic was picking up and the ghost kid bounced back and forth from one car.

"It's like volleyball!" Jill squealed in delight.

"Ha, ha, ha, ha." I laughed and clapped with each volley.

After about ten cars the road became quiet again and the ghost kid began to float back down to earth.

I pointed up and said, "Jill, does he look a little green to you?"

"Yes," she said. "I don't know if spooks can puke, but we better move out the way."

We backed up and watched him land. He was holding his stomach and started to open his mouth like he was going to toss some ghost cookies, so I gave him one more blast of the air horn. He screeched and spewed and sped off; leaving behind a long misty trail of ghost regurgitation in his wake. Jill and I laughed so hard we couldn't even stand. Revenge is sweet.

Unfortunately, my satisfaction was not destined to last very long. In fact, it barely lasted the weekend.

6 WATCH WHERE YOU SIT

Back at school on Monday morning the kid got me again. I wasn't even expecting it, but when I sat down in my desk, I sat right onto a sharp tack.

"Ye-ouch!" I jumped immediately back up, but it was too late, the tack had sunk deep.

"Ow Ow OW!" Pulling it out hurt just as much as it did going in.

"Hee ha, hee ha, hee ha ha ha ha."

Duke was floating in front of me on his back, laughing and stomping his feet against the air in pure pleasure.

I fruitlessly flung the tack at him and watched as it sailed right through him. He laughed again. Then completely satisfied by the results of his prank, he flew out of the window.

True to form the next morning, I discovered a tack on my seat. I picked it up, carried it over to the bulletin board and pushed it into the cork. I looked up and saw the ghost boy. He had a big frown on his face. I grinned back at him. He stuck out his tongue then flew out the window.

Again the next morning, I found a tack on my seat, and again I stuck it on the bulletin board. Duke left again disappointed.

He was certainly predictable, for on Thursday morning there was another tack on my seat. When I found it, he cried out, "No fair!" Then flew away.

By Friday morning he'd figured out that I wasn't going to be surprised by a tack ever again. So he came up with something new. As soon as I sat down in my desk, he slid into the seat beside me with such force that he knocked me out of my chair.

"Whoa!" I cried, flinging my arms out to break my fall, but I crashed right into Tony who sat in the desk next to mine.

"What the Hey!" He yelled, as I knocked him out of his desk and started a chain reaction.

Tony then fell into Marvin who sat next to him. Then like a row of human dominoes, Marvin fell into Debbie who fell into Jill. Jill, because she had noticed Dukey flying near the ceiling, was the only one who saw it coming and managed to stay in her desk.

Every kid in the class was laughing or shrieking, and Mr. Russell had a fit. He yelled for everyone to be quiet and for those of us still on the floor to get back in ours seats.

But, when I tried to get back into my seat, the ghost kid rushed over and jumped into my seat ahead of me. When I tried to sit down, he pushed me back out.

Mr. Russell gave me an irritated look and said, "Mr. Carson, get back in your seat, now!"

Once again I tried. I pushed and pushed, but could not get the ghost to budge. I kept glancing up at Mr. Russell who continued to glare at me. I was pushing so hard my face was turning red. Then I looked over at Jill. She wanted to help and was clearly frustrated. She stood up, pointed at the kid, and said, "But..., but,... but, he can't."

I caught her eye and shook my head for her to stop before she got in trouble too.

Then, all of a sudden, Dukey disappeared and I went flying across the seat and onto the floor on the other side of the desk. The whole class burst into laughter.

Everyone that is except for Mr. Russell, who said, "That's it, Corky. You have two more demerits. Now go stand in the hallway until you can remember how to sit at a desk."

Out in the hallway, I sat on the floor and put my face in my hands. Donkey Boy was waiting, and he brayed his annoying laugh for ten whole minutes before he finally got bored and left.

After school, Jill met up with me and we walked home together. Hanging with the best looking girl at school was cool. I guess there are some benefits to having a ghost kid annoy you every day.

"I've got something for you," she said.

"What?"

"Hold out your hand."

I did and she dropped a tack into it.

"Ha Ha,." I said sarcastically.

"No, we take it to that elf you told me about and get him to enchant it."

"He won't do it."

"Why not?"

"I asked him to enchant a stick for me, and he said he didn't enchant things for stupid humans."

"Then we'll just have to out smart him."

"But how?"

"I've got an idea."

Jill took a quick look around to make sure there weren't any ghost kids nearby and then we headed into the woods.

When we got to the old gnarly oak tree, she took the tack from me and pushed it into the dirt in front of the hole in the bottom of the tree. Then she knocked on the tree and said, "Oh, Mr. Elf are you home?"

A few seconds later he emerged from the hole. When Jill saw the tiny little man with the wrinkled face and hairy pointed ears, she jumped back and cried, "Oh!"

He looked at her then at me and said in that voice that was ten times bigger than he was, "You again. Didn't I tell you that if you woke me up again I would turn you into a mushroom?"

"But, it was me who woke you up," said Jill with a big smile. She dropped down into a squat and, said, "Hi my name is Jill." Then she offered him her hand.

The elf could only wrap his little hand around the tips of her fingers. As Jill shook his hand he just stared. He was just as bamboozled by her beauty as I was.

Jill said, "We were walking through the woods and saw that shiny thing on the ground in front of your door and wondered if you had lost a button."

"Button, hurrumph," he muttered as he picked up the tack. "It's not a button and it's not mine." He tossed it into the woods and I watched carefully where it landed.

"Sorry to have awakened you," Jill said. "We'll leave so you can get back to sleep."

He went back into his hole and I ran over to where he'd tossed the tack. It was right in the middle of a poison ivy patch. I hoped I wouldn't itch too much, because I knew exactly what I was going to do with that tack on Monday.

As Jill and I walked out of the woods, I asked, "Do you think your hand is enchanted now?"

"I sure hope so, but he only touched my fingertips on these three fingers."

"You probably won't be able to swat Duke into the next county, but maybe you can do a Three Stooges on him and poke him in the eyes."

Jill jabbed the air with two fingers and did the Curly cry, "Why you, why you... woob woob woob.... N'yuk, N'yuk, N'yuk!"

We both laughed all the way out of the woods.

* * * * *

I met up with Jill as she walked to school Monday morning.

"What if he does his invisibility thing this morning so that I can't see him?" I said.

"I think you can count on it."

"Why?"

"Because he wants to get you in trouble with Mr. Russell. He laughs the hardest when he causes you to get sent out of the room."

"But, you'll be able to see him."

"Sure, but I can't just yell out in class, 'Watch out Corky here comes the ghost.' I'll get in trouble too."

"What we need is a signal. Maybe you can tap a pencil on your desk when you see him."

"No, that will only annoy Mr. Russell and he'll tell me to stop and then I won't have a signal for you. We need something that I can do anytime and not get in trouble for it."

"Oh, I know. You can sneeze."

"I can't sneeze whenever I want to."

"But, you can fake a sneeze."

"Yeah, I can do that."

"OK, if you see the ghost in the classroom, sneeze once. If he's sitting in my seat, sneeze twice."

"And, if I see him flying fast toward your seat, I'll cough."

"That's great!"

"Ah-choo!"

"You see him?"

"No, I was just practicing."

When I arrived in the classroom, he was nowhere to be seen. I looked across the room to Jill, who shook her head to indicate that she didn't see him either. So things started out pretty quietly.

About halfway through the morning, Mr. Russell announced a pop-quiz in math. All of a sudden I heard Jill sneeze.

7 A GHOST MOBILE

Without looking up, I reached into my desk and got the enchanted thumb tack. I held it carefully by the point between two fingers. Now, I had to work quickly, or the Ghost Kid was going to do his annoying best to get me in trouble during the test.

I raised my other hand, and when Mr. Russell called on me, I asked, "May I sharpen my pencil."

"Hurry up." He said.

So, as I got up, I put my hand, with the tack between the fingers, on the seat. I acted like I was pushing out of my chair. What I was really doing was secretly leaving the tack, pointy side up, right where your left cheek meets the seat.

When I finished sharpening my pencil in the front of the room, I turned around and glanced at Jill. She looked up toward the light fixture to indicate where Dukey was hanging. I couldn't see him. But, assuming he was watching me, I looked up at the light fixture again then popped my eyes wide open like I had just seen him. Then I started running for my desk. Jill

started coughing like crazy. It was working.

I was two steps away from reaching my desk when Duke appeared. He wanted me to see the big satisfied grin on his face as he beat me there. I lunged forward and he slammed down into my seat just ahead of me. Perfection!

"YEOW!" That grin disappeared as his mouth opened wide in shock.

He shot out of my seat like a rocket and flew straight up through the ceiling. And, here's the best part. He could pass through the ceiling tile, but the tack couldn't. He was going so fast the tack rammed deep into the ceiling tile. And, pinned him there. He fell back through the ceiling and hung there. His pants were firmly attached to the ceiling.

He tried flying down, but the tack held him. He tried flying sideways, but no go. He screamed, "Let me go! Let me go!"

I started snickering. Mr. Russell, who was passing out the test, gave me a stare.

I looked over at Jill. She was rocking back and forth and her face was red as she held a hand over her mouth to keep in the laughter.

I looked back up and Dukey was flying around and around in a little circle going faster and faster until he looked like a ceiling fan. But, he couldn't break loose.

I bit my lip and snorted

Mr. Russell said, "Having a problem there, Mr. Carson."

I coughed and said, "Uh, no sir, just a little something caught in my throat."

"Do you need to go get some water?"

"Yes, sir."

As I walked out of the classroom door, I heard the ghost boy scream, "MOMMEEE!"

I quickly shut the door, and howled in laughter all the way to the water fountain. What a great Monday this was turning out to be.

For the rest of the day, whenever I wanted a chuckle, all I had to do was look up. And, there was Dukey hanging by the seat of his pants. Pulling at the tack. Sometimes he was swirling around. A big ghost mobile.

The next morning he was gone, but his pants weren't. He'd wriggled out of his pants and gone home with a bare bottom. That was funny. I wished I'd been there to see it.

The following morning, the pants were gone, but not completely. He'd ripped them away, but the tack was still there. And, for the rest of the year I could always look up see a little piece of ghost fabric hanging by that tack. That always brought a smile to my face. But, as usual, it didn't take long for Dukey to recover. He was back to bugging me within days. This time he got me where it really hurt.

8 BENCHED!

I was at basketball practice when all of sudden I couldn't hit a basket to save my life. But, there was something weird about the way I was missing. The ball wasn't bouncing off the rim or the backboard and not going in; it was veering off in mid-air as if a gust of wind was blowing it off course. But, there was no wind inside the gymnasium. I began to suspect ghosts and wished Jill was around to spot him for me.

It wasn't long before the coach noticed. "Having a tough day, Carson?"

"Just a little slow getting warmed up, Coach." I replied.

"Since you're not getting any baskets, I want you to pass to Mumford and let him take the shots."

Oh no, not Mumford. He was my arch rival on the team, and almost as annoying as the ghost kid. "But, Coach!"

"We're playing the first place team in one week. Either make shots, pass to Mumford or sit on the bench."

"Yes, sir."

That's when I finally heard him, "He-ha, he-ha, he-ha ha ha ha."

I looked around, but still couldn't see him. The coach tossed me the ball and said, "Take the ball in and pass to Mumford." So, I took the ball, dribbled to center court, side-stepped the opposing forward and made a beautiful bounce pass to Mumford who was perfectly positioned under the basket. Except the ball never made it to him. It bounced right where I wanted it to, but then it suddenly swerved out of bounds.

Mumford yelled, "Can't you pass either?"

I glanced at the coach who gave me a scowling look. Then I heard donkey boy braying from somewhere up near the ceiling. This was not going well. I had to do something quick, or I was going to be warming the bench. I took the ball in again. This time I yelled, "Mumford!" and feinted toward him, then I leaped spinning into the air and shot toward the basket. "This better work." I hoped.

It did. The ball dropped right in - a perfect shot!

"Woo-Hoo!" I yelled. Mumford stuck his tongue out at me, and at the same instant something slammed into my back and knocked me face down onto the court.

I rolled over and saw Duke. He said, "That's only going to work once!" Then he grinned and disappeared again.

I took the ball in once again, this time I feinted toward Mumford, spun in the air, then passed the ball behind my back to him. He wasn't expecting the ball, but it was a perfect pass and hit him in the chest. He grabbed it before it got away, jumped and made the basket.

"Woo-Hoo!" I yelled, then ducked. I saw the bottom of Duke's feet as he flew over me and through the floor.

"Woo-Hoo!" I yelled again, and everybody in the gym turned around and looked at me like I was weird. I shrugged and took my place back on the court, and thought, "This day might work out after all."

But, I was wrong. You can only fool a ghost so many times. From then on, he just hovered near my head, and every time I tried to shoot or pass he just reached out and tipped the ball and I would miss. Ten minutes later, the coach put me on the bench for the rest of practice. And ghost boy flew in circles around my head laughing.

"Don't you have anyone else to haunt?" I grumbled.

"No, just you. Hee ha, hee ha, hee ha."

With me sitting on the bench, he had nothing to do. Eventually he got bored, and that was when he did think of someone else to annoy. Jill.

9 BUBBLE BOY

The next morning in class, Jill came up to me and said, "Someone came in my house and ate all the middles."

"The middles?"

"You know, the middle of the Oreo cookies."

"The white stuff?"

"Yes, it's the best part. And, when I got the package out yesterday all the middles were gone. There was just the chocolate cookie outsides.

"Maybe the factory made a mistake."

"No, there were little teeth marks leaving little trails of white stuff on the inside of the cookies."

"The Ghost Kid! It has to be."

"Yes, now he knows where I live, he's probably going to haunt me all the time. I'll never have whole Oreos ever again."

"We'll have to fix that."

"It won't do any good to hide them," Jill looked forlorn. "He'll find them."

"Maybe we can disguise them. Make them look like vegetables or something."

"If only we knew what he didn't like."

"We need to come up with something that everybody hates the taste of."

"Yeah, something nasty like beets or liver. Then I could hide the Oreos in a bag of beets or something."

"My uncle likes both those things," I lamented. "What if Dukey likes them too?"

"Then it can't be food because no matter how yucky it is there will always be at least one weirdo who likes it. And that ghost kid is really weird."

"Can you remember tasting anything that was really gross that you weren't supposed to taste?'

"I once tasted the potted paste in art class, but it actually tasted pretty good."

"Yeah, I tasted that stuff, too. Hey, I know a good idea. Instead of trying to disguise the cookies as something gross, we could refill all those Oreos he ate the filling out of with white paste. Then he'll think you got a new package and eat the paste, and glue his mouth shut!"

"Oh, that's a great idea. Let's do it!"

"I can just see it," I laughed. "Dukey sneaks into your kitchen when we're at school and eats all that paste. Then his lips and teeth will get all stuck together. It ought to shut up that donkey laugh for a long long time. I just wish we could be here to watch it!"

Then Jill said, "It won't work."

"Why not?"

"The paste will harden and the chocolate outsides will stick together and he won't be able to pry them apart."

"Oh, yeah."

* * * * *

Later that day at lunch, I sat with Jill.

"Hey, I got a new idea while I was in the bathroom. We put soap in the cookies!"

"You mean that squishy stuff we use to wash our hands in the bathroom?"

"No, that's too runny. We need to get a bar of white soap and melt it on the stove in a pot. Maybe add a little water to help soften it."

"We can put it in my Mom's pastry decorating bag and squeeze it right onto the cookies."

"Won't she get mad?"

"It's soap. It'll be like we're cleaning it."

"Yeah. Okay."

After school we went over to Jill's house. While I melted some Ivory soap in a pan on the stove, Jill kept a lookout for the annoying ghost kid.

Once it was nice and creamy, I said, "How's it look?"

"It looks just like cookie filling to me," said Jill, "but, it still smells like soap. Let's add some vanilla to mask the smell."

"That's a good idea. I think we should add some sugar too. That way it will taste sweet and he won't know he's eating soap until it's too late."

"Then we better put in lots of sugar."

We took the mixture and poured it into the pastry decorating bag. Jill watched for Duke, while I laid out the cookies then squeezed a little bit onto all the bottoms. Then I put the tops on them and pressed the two chocolate pieces together.

When I finished, I said, "They look good enough to eat."

"They sure do," said Jill. "Let's put them back into the package."

Toward the end of school the next day, I heard Jill sneeze. I looked up and saw the ghost boy hovering around the ceiling. I was wondering what prank he was going to pull, when he disappeared. Jill sneezed twice. That was supposed to mean he was sitting in my desk, but I was sitting in it. Then I saw the letter "D" appear on my desk. Next the letter "U" appeared beside it. Then the letter "K." He was writing his name on my desk. Once he'd written the letter "E," he started up his donkey laugh. He swirled around the room laughing. I picked up my pencil, and erased it.

Jill coughed. He must be flying right toward me at full speed. I ducked but he wasn't trying to hit me. He had a pencil in his hand and started to write his name again. But before he could finish the bell rang. School's out. I jumped up and yelled across the room, "Hey, Jill. Did your Mom buy you some more Oreos?"

"Yes."

"Then let's go to your house and eat some."

I heard the pencil hit the floor. Ghost boy was gone.

We grabbed our books and ran. When we got near Jill's house we slowed down.

I said, "Let's sneak up to the kitchen window and peak in."

As we peered in the window, we saw dozens of chocolate cookie pieces on the floor. They were flying out of the pantry. Duke was eating as fast as he could and flinging the chocolate part over his shoulder as he finished each one. With each one he ate he laughed out loud, "Hee ha!" All we could see was his back. It appeared that he was really enjoying the soapy mixture. Finally he finished and turned around, and it was our turn to laugh. White soap suds were spilling out of his mouth like an overflowing washing machine. A white froth covered his face from his nose to his neck and from ear to ear. We ran inside.

When he saw us he proclaimed, "I ate your favorite part of the cookie again. Hee ha, hee ha, hee ha, hee ha ha ha ha!"

As he laughed more bubbles, these the size of grapes, came out of his mouth.

We burst out laughing."

"What are you laughing at? I'm the one that ate the cookie cream."

I was laughing so hard, I couldn't speak. All I could do was point at him.

"Look, it's Santa Claus!" shouted Jill.

I caught my breath and said, "Hey, Ghost Boy, you need a shave."

"Don't laugh at me!" he cried. But when he opened his mouth more bubbles came out, and we laughed even harder.

"He's foaming at the mouth. It's not a ghost it's a rabid dog! Quick call the Pound."

Jill called, "Here doggy. Woof! Woof! Woof!"

"Don't laugh at me!" He screamed.

More bubbles shot out of his mouth and flew in front of his face.

"Wh-what is that?" He cried.

"It's not Ghost Boy anymore, it's Bubble Boy!" I taunted.

"MOMMEEEE... hic... hic... hic!

Oh, this was great. Now he had the hiccups. And with each one, the bubbles burst out of his nose. Then the bubbles in his nose must have tickled because he sneezed and two long streams of white foam shot out of his nose.

"He's a soap dispenser." Chortled Jill.

"Or a can of shaving cream!" I added.

"Stop it! Stop it!" Duke wailed.

Then he started to turn green and we heard a rumbling from his stomach. When he opened his mouth I thought he was going to puke. But, then he burped. It was the longest and loudest burp I'd ever heard, and as it came out, so did a bubble. A big bubble. It came out of his mouth and got bigger and bigger and bigger until suddenly it engulfed his head.

"Now he looks like he's wearing a spaceman helmet!" I exclaimed.

He tried to pop it. But it was too thick. His finger would just dent it or go through it, but it would not break. He started thrashing at it with both hands. It still wouldn't break, but it did create more bubbles, smaller ones that stuck on the outside of the bigger one.

"Look, look Corky, now he has bubble hair growing on his bubble head," Jill howled. We laughed so hard we couldn't stand. Dukey finally got disgusted and flew away. It was the best prank ever. It was so much fun, we thought maybe we could try it on some living people one day... or maybe not.

10 MAGIC FINGERS

The next day when I arrived in class, Mr. Russell was standing beside my desk and looking down at it. When I got there I saw what he was looking at. Duke had written his name all over my desktop. He must've written it 100 times.

Mr. Russell said, "This your new nickname?"

"Uh, no, sir. I didn't write all that."

"Maybe not, but you'll be the one erasing it. I want all this off by the end of the day."

I pulled out my big Pink Pearl eraser and started to work.

"99 more to go," I grumbled.

But, as I started to erase the second one, the first one appeared again. I erased the second one faster, but before I could erase another he'd rewritten the last one. I tried covering it with my hand, but when I moved my hand, he'd rewritten it – through my hand. That was when he started he-hawing. And, as he laughed a few soap suds dropped onto the floor beside me. That was why he wasn't appearing. He didn't want me to see his foamy beard.

Never the less, he was getting the better of me. If I didn't get those names erased by day's end, I was probably going to end up with some demerits or worse - detention! Clearly I was going to have to out-think the ghost boy once again. Then he started laughing harder. I looked down at my desk and started seeing even more signatures appear. He was writing more of them. More I needed to erase and more he wasn't going to let me erase. If Mr. Russell saw these new ones, I was surely going to get blamed for them.

"Darn it, Dukey!" I said aloud.

"Don't you call me that!" He exclaimed.

And, with that exclamation I got an idea. I grabbed my pencil and started adding the letter "Y" to each one of his signatures.

"Hey stop that!" He cried.

He snatched my pink pearl and started erasing the "Ys", but I could write them faster than he could erase them.

I started chanting in a soft whisper only he could hear, "Dukey... Dukey... Dukey... Dukey... Dukey..."

It wasn't long before I had added a "Y" to every signature on the desk. Then as soon as he finished erasing one, I'd put it right back. Eventually he got tired and left.

Later on, when we returned from lunch, I saw that he had erased every single "Y." So, I put them all back. It only took a minute.

I still couldn't see him, but I did hear him yell, "MOMMEEEE!"

When we went out to recess, I hoped my plan was going to work. It did. When I came back, he had erased every single signature.

But, he wasn't finished with me for the day. After school at basketball practice, he wouldn't let me get off a single shot or a pass. Once again, I was put on the bench. Duke, of course, was circling above me braying his donkey laugh, but making things worse was Mumford who made a point of dribbling by me and snickering every few minutes. I was furious. This was really getting to me. There was nothing I loved more than basketball and the annoying ghost kid was successfully keeping me from it. The way things were going, Coach wasn't going to let me play in the big game on Saturday. I had to do something.

When practice was over I went over to the equipment room and checked out a tennis racquet. I stormed out of the school and headed down the sidewalk toward the woods. Halfway there, I ran into Jill who was out riding her bike.

"Hi Corky. Where are you going in such a hurry?"

"It's that darn ghost kid; he's ruining my basketball game. I'm sick of it; I need some way to fight back. So, I'm going to see the old elf and ask him to enchant this racquet! "

"Oh no, Corky, you can't just ask him; you have to trick him. What are you going to say?"

"I don't know. I'll offer to do chores for him. Maybe I'll just beg and plead, but I've got to get some help. That ghost has been tormenting me for weeks, and I can't take it anymore. And, now, when he's not bothering me, he's bothering you."

When we walked by the haunted house, Jill pointed toward it and said, "Isn't that your cat?"

I looked over and saw Joey chasing a rat out of a basement window.

"Hey Joey. Joey!"

He stopped chasing the rat and walked over to me. I reached down and rubbed his head and said, "What are you doing chasing rats? Don't I give you enough to eat at home?"

"Bbrrrt!" he said.

"I can't go home and feed you now; I've got to go see the elf. I'll feed you when I get home. I promise!"

"Bbrrrt." he said, and rubbed up against my legs.

"That's a good boy." I said.

Jill and I started walking again and Joey followed us. When I reached the path leading into the woods, I said. "Wish me luck."

"Don't you want me to come with you?" Jill asked.

"No. I'll be fine. Just make sure Joey doesn't follow me. Who knows what the elf might do if he sees a cat."

"OK, I'll take him home. Good luck. I hope you don't get turned into a mushroom."

"Oh, you don't really believe he can do that do you?"

"A few weeks ago I didn't believe in ghosts or elves."

"Well, if I'm not back in half an hour..."

"Then what?"

"I guess I'll be pizza topping."

"Not funny, Corky!"

I headed down into the woods. When I got to the old gnarled tree, I knocked on it near the hole. A few moments later the elf walked out rubbing his eyes.

"Who is out here waking me up?" He growled.

"Just me, Mr. Elf. I was wondering if you would enchant this..."

All of a sudden I was looking up at the elf instead of down at him. And, I couldn't move. I also couldn't make a sound. I could see the tennis racquet on the ground in front of me and it looked really big. The elf bent over and peered at me, then said in his deep gravelly voice, "Stupid human, I told you if you annoyed me I would turn you into a mushroom."

Then he went back into his hole.

I don't know how much time passed, but I could see the sun getting lower in the sky. I really started to worry. What if I'm still out here when it gets dark? What if some animal comes along and tries to eat me? Will it hurt? If I'm late for dinner, my parents are going to get really mad.

After a while I heard something walking behind me. I hoped it was a meat-eating carnivore and not a mushroom-eating vegetarian. Then I heard Jill calling, "Corky... Corky..."

I saw her pick up the tennis racquet and say, "Oh no, Corky."

She crouched down and looked at me, and said, "Corky is that you? Are you a mushroom?"

Just then the elf came back out of his hole. "Who is making all the noise out here?"

Jill dropped the racquet, turned to him, and said with a bright cheery voice, "Hi Mr. Elf. Do you like Skittles?"

She held her hand out to him. In it were three candies: one purple, one red and one orange.

"What are these, more buttons?" He growled.

"No, you eat 'em. Taste one; they're delicious."

He took the red one and popped it into his mouth. All of a sudden he started smiling.

"That's good." He took the orange one.

"That's good, too." He took the purple one.

"That's very good. You got any more?"

"I might," she said, "I'll have to look. But, I was wondering, have you seen my friend Corky?"

"You mean that bothersome boy?"

"He was probably asking you to enchant that tennis racquet."

"Yeah, I turned him into a mushroom."

"This one?" She asked pointing at me.

"Yes."

"Will you turn him back?"

"Don't need to, he'll turn back on his own."

"That's great! When?"

"About a hundred years."

"A hundred years! That's too long. Can't you turn him back now? You can have these."

Jill held out six Skittles.

"None of those are purple."

"Oh, you like the purple ones."

Jill dug around in the Skittles bag for a few moments, then she held out a small bag of Martha White All-Purpose Flour, and said, "Would you mind holding this for me? I'm going to need both hands to find you some purple ones."

The elf took the bag, and Jill continued her search.

After a few moments she held out her hand again. There were six purple Skittles in her palm.

"Here you go."

He took the candy and handed back the flour. Suddenly I was a human again.

Jill turned around and put her finger over her lips – signaling me that I needed to keep my mouth shut. Then she turned around and dropped something on the ground in front of the elf.

"Oops." She said.

The elf looked down at what appeared to be a tape dispenser.

"I'm trying to get another handful of Skittles for you, and I can't pick that up," Jill said. "Would you mind handing that to me, so that I don't drop any of your candy."

The elf picked up the tape and held it out for her. She took the tape and then placed a dozen Skittles into his little palm.

"Thanks, Mr. Elf. We'll see you around. Corky, grab your tennis racquet; it's time to go."

As we walked out of the woods, I whispered, “So, what’s with the tape and the flour? Why didn’t you get him to touch my tennis racquet?”

“Look where asking him to touch the tennis racquet got you. We’d have made a fine pair of mushrooms for the next 100 years. Besides there are so many things you can do with tape. Here, you take it.”

Jill handed me the tape and added, “It’s double-stick, that means it’s sticky on both sides of the tape.”

“That means double the fun when it comes to getting back at the annoying ghost kid.”

“Think of something good to use it for, and I’ll see you at school tomorrow.

“But, what about the flour.”

“That you’ll have to wait and see.”

We were back at the street and it was time to take our separate directions toward our homes. I held up my hand and said, “I’ll see ya. And, uh, thanks for saving my life back there.”

“It was nothing. Besides, I got him to touch my thumb. Now on one hand, my thumb and three fingers are enchanted. You know what that means?”

“What?” I asked.

“It means, I’m going to start wearing a ponytail again!”

"Huh?"

"You'll see."

11 GHOST CATCHER

The next morning as I stood outside our classroom door, I saw Jill walking down the hallway toward me. Her ponytail was back just as she promised and it was swinging back and forth with every step she took. All of a sudden the ghost kid came flying out of the ceiling right behind Jill. He was making a beeline for her ponytail.

"Jill!" I hollered. "Dukey at six o'clock."

She smiled and gave me a thumbs up.

A second later the ghost kid was on her.

"I got-cha now!" He laughed as he grabbed her ponytail.

"Ow!" Jill cried, "Let go."

Of course that guaranteed that he wouldn't let go. Which was just what Jill wanted. She took her head and swung it around in a circle. The ghost kid was hanging on tight.

"Wheee!" He yelled. "Swing me again."

Jill swung him again, but as he came around in front of her face, she reached out with her enchanted fingers and grabbed the top of his underwear sticking out of his shorts. Then she gave it a hard yank, pulling his underwear right up to his neck.

"Wedgie!" She yelled.

Duke immediately let go of her hair, but Jill wasn't letting go of him so easily. She swung him around and around stretching his underwear almost enough to cover his head.

"Let me go!" He cried.

"Sure thing Donkey Boy." She started swinging him faster and faster, finally flinging him toward the wall where he vanished out of sight.

I was laughing so loud, Mr. Russell came outside to see what was going on.

"What are you laughing at Carson?"

"Uh, Jill, sir. She was doing something funny."

He looked at Jill and said, "Perhaps you can share your comedy with the entire class."

"I hope to very soon." She replied.

"Well, it's time to take your seats. Come on inside."

As Jill walked in the door, I whispered, "What do you mean; you hope to very soon?"

"I'll tell you later. Have you decided what you're going to do with the double stick tape?"

"I sure have, but I'm going to need your help. Can you cut lunch?"

"Sure."

"Great! Meet me out on the sidewalk in front of the woods."

"I'll see you there."

* * * * *

I met up with Jill in front of the school, and we headed down the sidewalk toward the woods.

"Is he anywhere around?" I asked.

"No, I think that wedgie is going to keep him occupied for a while."

"Well, keep a look out anyway. If he finds out about this, it won't work."

"What are you going to do?"

"I'm going to build a ghost trap with the double stick tape."

"I can't wait to see that! Hey, why are you stopping here?"

"There's a path into the woods right beside the haunted house."

"Oh, no. Look it's Joey!"

I looked where she was pointing. Joey was standing in the window on the third floor with a rat in his mouth.

"Joey! Joey!" I called.

"Joey, Joey!" Jill and I called together.

Finally he came scurrying out of the basement window and ran up to me. He dropped the rat at my feet. The rat tried to run away, but Joey planted a paw on his back holding him.

"No, no Joey. Let that poor little guy go."

Joey lifted his paw and the rat disappeared into the tall grass.

"Let's go into the woods right here," I said.

"But, it's so thick here." Jill said, "Why don't we go down a little further and use the path?"

"That's why this is going to work. Push through the branches and underbrush here. Just on the other side I've created a new path."

"Okay, I'll try it, but.... Wow, it's like a tunnel in here!"

"Yeah, I had to hack away the branches and trample the undergrowth for about 30 feet.

"There's just barely enough room for me to stand up."

"That's on purpose. It's long and narrow and leads right to my trap."

"Where's that?"

"Just beyond where I stopped clearing. Come on, I'll show you." I pulled a branch aside so that she could get through.

"Why'd you stop clearing here."

"So he won't notice the trap. See these two small trees that are growing about two feet apart. I'm going to wind the tape between them and make a net."

"But how do you get through the net? It's too thick in here to go around it."

"I'm going to leave an opening at the bottom about a foot high that I can slide under."

"You better hurry, we've only got 20 minutes of lunch left."

Starting about 12 inches from the ground, I wound the tape tightly between the two trees. I went around and around as high as I could reach.

"Okay that's it. If I'm lucky this will work like fly paper."

"Better make it higher," Jill said, "just to be sure."

"I don't have anything to stand on."

"Then I'll do it, but you'll have to hold me piggyback so I can reach."

I held Jill and tried to keep from falling as she wound the tape even higher between the trees.

"Okay That's enough," she declared. "Besides I need to save some of this tape for something else."

"What?"

"Tell you later, we've got to run; lunchtime is over."

* * * * *

After school that day I put Operation Ghost Trap into action. I went to basketball practice early and started taking practice shots. I hoped Wedgie Boy would arrive early looking for some revenge. I wasn't disappointed. I only made two shots before the ball started mysteriously veering away from the basket. Since it was practice and not a game, all the backboards and baskets had been lowered. So, I faked like I was shooting for the basket in front of me, then I turned to my left and shot the side court basket.

"Two points!" I yelled to the empty gym.

I retrieved the ball and started to fake again but the basketball lifted right out of my hands.

"Hee ha, hee ha, hee ha ha ha ha." Duke appeared above me holding the ball.

I stuck out my tongue, then said, "Nah, nah, you can't hit me!"

He threw the ball right at me. I caught it. "Ha ha, yourself!"

I shot toward the nearest basket. He flew after it and grabbed it before it went in. Then he came flying at me full force. I turned and bent over and let him hit me with the ball.

"Hey, cut it out." I cried.

"Hee ha, hee ha!"

I stuck my tongue out and gave him raspberries, "Pbbbbbbtttt!" Then I yelled, "Hey, Wedgie Boy, you can't catch me." And, I ran out of the gym.

I charged down the hallway and slammed out the double-door to the parking lot. I stopped and scooped up a pile of acorns I'd left by the curb. When Duke came through the door behind me, I threw the acorns at him. Of course they went right through him, and he laughed. But, I ignored him and took off running down the sidewalk and toward the woods. I'd only gotten ten feet before I felt the first acorn hit me. So, I stopped and dodged the next two.

"Ha ha, you can't hit me!" Then I sing-songed, "Wedgie Boy... Wedgie Boy!"

He threw another and I let it hit me. "Ouch!" He can sure throw hard for a dead guy.

I turned to run again when something really hard hit me in the back of the head. I reached back and rubbed the sore spot. It was bleeding. He was throwing rocks. I started running really fast in a zig zag pattern so that he was less likely to hit me. I dodged behind trees and telephone poles.

Finally, I reached the haunted house and turned off into the woods. As I ran along beside the house, I saw Joey through a first floor window. "Darn it." I thought, but there's nothing I can do about it now. So, I ducked through the underbrush and slowed down just long enough to make sure Duke was following. A rocked whizzed past my head and I took off down the leaf-lined tunnel as fast as I could go.

Suddenly I was afraid my plan was going to fail because he was flying so close to me that he yelled right in my ear, "I'm going to get you Corky and then I'm going to get your girlfriend too!"

At that moment I was at the end of the trail, so I hit the ground in my best baseball slide. Just like I was sliding home under the catcher's mitt, I threw my legs forward and my arms back and slid right underneath my sticky tape trap. But, I didn't stop on the other side. There was a steep slope I hadn't noticed before and I kept going. My trap was at the top of a steep hill and I was going down the other side. The leaves underneath me were wet and slippery. I was going faster and faster, completely out of control. I tried to dig my heels in but they wouldn't grip. Luckily I was able to use my hands as rudders and steered away from a couple of trees I would've crashed into. Finally I reached the bottom of the hill and came to a stop. I looked back up the hill. I must've gone 100 feet.

I stood up and brushed the leaves off my gym clothes. I didn't see the ghost kid anywhere. I had no idea if my trap worked or not. Then I heard the sweetest sound in the world.

"Let me go! Get me out of here. MOMMEEEE!"

When I got to the top of the hill, those two little trees were shaking like a gale wind was blowing them. The ghost kid was very stuck. His clothes were completely attached, but he wasn't going to wriggle out of his pants like he did that time with the tack. His bare legs, arms, hands, face and hair were all firmly stuck into a wall of sticky tape. The more he tried to get free, the more he got himself stuck.

I stood there and smiled. I was too tired to laugh.

He looked at me and pleaded, "Come on Corky, let me go!"

I shook my head and said, "Maybe in a few days, Duke, but I've only got two more practices before the big game on Saturday. And, because of you I've got to prove to the coach that I can still play basketball."

"No fair, Corky. No Fair!"

"Hey, look at it this way, Duke. All I'm doing is what your parents should have done 70 years ago."

"What's that?"

"Put you in Time-Out!"

12 BAD IDEA

On Saturday night I got to play in the big game. I even scored 12 points. Monday morning it was back to school. It was a gloomy cloudy day and I could hear thunder in the distance. Rain was on the way. On our way to school, Jill and I stopped by the woods. Dukey was just like I left him.

"Nice work, Corky." Jill said.

"Yeah, I just wish I could take a picture of him and show everybody so they wouldn't think I was crazy. But, I know nothing would show up on the film. Say, maybe if we used some of that fl..."

"Shhhh!" Jill hissed and shook her head.

Duke heard us and whined, "Are you guys going to let me down? It's scary out here at night."

"What have you got to be afraid of - you're a ghost!" I said.

"Well, it's lonely."

"If I let you go, will you promise to stop annoying Jill and me?"

"Yes, yes, I promise."

I didn't really believe him, but for some reason I felt sorry for him.

BOOM! There was a loud crack of thunder very near by. Jill screamed and Dukey cried out, "Hurry!"

"OK, OK. Jill, do you have any scissors in your book bag?"

"Yes."

"Then, let's cut him down."

"Let me try to pull him off first with my enchanted hand." She grabbed him by the back of his pants and started to pull.

"Ow, ow, ow. You're hurting me." Duke whimpered.

"Oh, this hurts me much more than it hurts you," Jill said with a wicked grin on her face. Then she grabbed the wrist of her enchanted hand with her other hand and yanked as hard as she could. There was a loud ripping sound as Duke came free.

"YEEEEOWWWW!" he screamed.

Jill had a very satisfied smile on her face.

"I'm going to get you for this!" Duke yelled.

"Uh, uh, uh... Don't forget your promise." I said.

"I had my fingers crossed so it doesn't count. Hee ha, hee ha, hee ha ha ha ha!"

Jill reached out to snatch him, but he ducked out of her reach then flew away.

"I told you this was a bad idea." She said.

"I wanted to give him a chance."

"That little boy is just mean!"

"Well, we better get to school before the bell rings."

"Hey, do you smell smoke?"

"Yeah, and it looks like it's coming from the haunted house."

13 TRUCE!

I ran up the path and saw the old house was burning. The roof was on fire.

"It must have been struck by lightening." I said. "We better call the fire department."

"Oh, no!" Jill cried, and pointed towards the upstairs window. "It's your cat."

I looked up and saw Joey in a window on the third floor. "Joey, Joey!" I called.

He just stood there and cried. I could hear him through the broken glass. "Meow, meow, meow." It was a very sad sound.

"He's afraid," I cried. "I have to go get him."

"You can't," Jill said, "it's too dangerous!"

"I have to or he'll die."

I ran over to the broken basement window that I'd seen Joey come out of. I kicked out the rest of the glass, then I lowered myself into the basement. It was dark, but there was just enough light for me to make out the stairs. I ran up the stairs to the first floor, then I had to look around to find the next stair case. It was around the corner, I ran up to the second floor. Then around to the last staircase. I ran up to the third floor. I could feel the heat from the fire coming out of the ceiling. Smoke was seeping down from above and I had to duck to breathe. Bent over at the waist, I ran down the hallway. I was getting confused. I couldn't figure out which room Joey was in.

"Joey, Joey!" I called. Finally, I heard his meow. I ran into the room and grabbed him. I turned to run back out.

CRASH! I heard a loud noise from the hallway. I ran to the door and looked out. The ceiling had collapsed right over the stair case. I was trapped. I ran to the window and yelled out of the broken pane, "Help! Help! I'm trapped. Smoke was now even lower in the room and I had to squat down on the floor. I could see Jill running away screaming, "Help! Fire! Corky is trapped!"

Holding Joey tight in my arms, I turned around and screamed. I saw a face in front of me. Then I recognized it. It was Duke.

"Quick, follow me." he said.

"No!" I said.

"I'll show you a way out."

"No, you're just trying to trick me."

"If you don't come with me you'll die."

"Well, isn't that what you want? "

"No, I never wanted you to get killed."

"What about the time you scared me so bad I jumped backwards into the street and almost got hit by a car."

"I'm sorry, Corky that was an accident; I didn't know you could jump so far."

"But, you kept scaring me that way."

"Yeah, but I always waited until there weren't any cars coming."

"Gee, thanks a lot."

"Come on, let's go!"

"No, I don't trust you. I still think you're trying to kill me."

"Corky, I don't want to kill you. I mean, if you were dead, who would I play jokes on?"

"I'm sure you'd find somebody else."

"Corky, I don't want you to be dead, because then you'd be a ghost too."

"So, why would you care?"

"Cause, you'd be a bigger ghost than me. And, if you're bigger than me... Well, just think of all the mean things you could do to me!"

Corky couldn't help grinning.

"So, I want you to stay alive. That way, I get to keep playing jokes on you and you can't come after me and get even!"

"OK you got a point, but how are you going to help me. It looks like the only thing I can do is jump out of the window and even though you can fly, you're not strong enough to keep me from falling. I'll still die."

"Just follow me, Corky."

I stared at him. I didn't know what to do. The smoke was even lower and it was beginning to hurt my throat.

Suddenly, Duke grabbed my shirt and yelled, "Come on. Now!"

I started crawling in the direction he pulled me. I held Joey tight against my chest and crawled with one hand.

Duke led me back into the hallway where the ceiling was completely on fire. He pulled me to the wall. There was a small metal door in the wall. He pulled it open and said, "Get in."

He started pushing my butt. I stuck my head into the dark hole, and said, "I can't see anything."

"Trust me..." then he added, "just this once." Then he picked up my feet and shoved. I fell forward, then suddenly I was sliding. It was a chute. A laundry chute. I slid around and around and around; faster and faster in a long spiral. I came to an abrupt halt as I smashed into some stinky moldy cloth. At least it was soft. Before I could get up, Duke was pulling me up. It was dark and I could still smell the smoke. He guided me to the basement window where I came in. I put Joey on the window sill and let him go. He ran off. Then, I started to pull myself up, but it was too high. I could feel my feet sliding against the wall. There wasn't anything I could put my foot on to help me climb up.

A loud noise erupted behind me. It sounded like the roof caved in. I turned around and looked and a huge pile of burning embers came sliding down the laundry chute.

"Hurry!" cried Duke.

I tried running up the wall, but gravity was keeping me down. I jumped, but I couldn't go high enough. I started coughing from all the smoke.

"Stand on my back," Duke said.

"It won't work; my foot will go right through you."

"Not if I don't want it to."

I stepped onto his back and was amazed. He felt like a real boy. I pushed off his back and was able to climb out the window.

I stood up and ran toward the street just as the fire truck pulled up. Jill was running behind the truck along with dozens of neighbors from all over the block.

"Everyone keep back!" ordered the Fire Chief as his men spilled out of the truck.

I started walking home, but the Chief grabbed me by the shoulder. "Were you in that house?"

"I was rescuing my cat."

"You leave the rescuing to us. Fires are extremely dangerous, and can kill you very quickly. Stay away from them!"

"Yes, sir." I said, and turned toward my house.

"Don't you want to stay and watch the fire?" asked Jill.

"No, I just want to go home, put Joey inside the house and change clothes. Besides, we have to get to school."

"OK, I'll walk with you."

"OW!" I yelped as something hit my head.

"What is it?" Jill asked.

I turned around and there was Duke tossing an acorn up and down in his hand.

"Why don't you give us a break!" Jill yelled.

"Hey, just because I saved Corky's life doesn't mean I like you guys."

He reared back his arm to throw and Jill struck like a snake. I've never seen her move so fast. She snatched him by the ear with her enchanted fingers and held him tight and said, “If you don’t leave Corky alone today, I’m going to swing you by your ear. I’ll make you hurt so bad you’ll think you’re still alive!”

“OK, OK, I promise.”

“Oh, I know what your promise is worth... nothing!”

“Please Corky!” he appealed to me.

I looked in his eyes and I could tell he meant it. His eyes looked just like they did when he helped me in the fire. “You can let him go, Jill.”

“Bad decision.” She said, but let him go.

“He haw, he haw, he haw haw haw. It’s just until tomorrow!”

14 EXPOSED!

Duke was as good as his word. The next day when we arrived in class, we could see that he had been busy. He had written my name all over my desk, at least 20 times, but he had spelled it: Corkee. He had done the same to Jill's desk except he spelled her name: Jil.

Mr. Russell saw it immediately and came over to my desk. "Corky, haven't we already talked about writing your name on your desk?"

"But, sir, that isn't even how I spell my name!"

He looked a little closer, when suddenly a piece of paper fell out of my notebook onto the desk. On it was written: 'Mr. Rusel is Stupid.' I could see that the "S" was written in reverse.

Mr Rusel is Stupid

"Mr. Carson, what is the meaning of this!" He yelled.

"But, sir, this looks like it was written by a first grader."

"Then why was it in your notebook?"

"I don't know sir, it..."

"BURRRRRPPP!"

The class burst into laughter, and Mr. Russell said, "Mr. Carson, don't be disrespectful."

"It wasn't me..."

"BURRRRRPPP!"

The class laughed again.

"That's it, you're going to detention!"

"But, Mr. Russell," Jill called out from the other side of the room, "it's not Corky. Look, somebody wrote all over my desk, too! Ow! Ow! Ow!"

Jill suddenly reached back and grabbed her ponytail just above the rubber bands. Her ponytail looked stiff as a board and stood straight up in the air. With a determined look on her face, Jill pulled her head forward, then immediately her head jerked backward. Forward again then backward. Back and forth, back and forth, to the class it looked like she was doing some odd dance. I was the only one that knew that her ponytail was the rope in a spooky game of tug-of-war. To finally win, she bent over at the waist really hard and her ponytail snapped back over her face. She stood upright and it fell back to her shoulders. She then turned around and appeared to be grabbing frantically at thin air.

"What is going on in my classroom!" shouted Mr. Russell.

"Sir, it's haunt..."

"BURRRRRPPP!"

"Jill sit down in your desk this minute!"

"Yes, sir."

As she slid into her desk, Duke body-slammed her and she went flying right out the other side and onto the floor.

The whole class gasped.

Jill was still the only one who could see him, but I could hear his annoying laugh.

"Hee ha, hee ha, hee ha ha ha ha."

Mr. Russell bellowed, "Miss Warbler, I said in your seat!"

Jill stood up and brushed off her dress. Then she walked around her desk to get in from the left hand side. I could see that she was watching something as she tried to slide back into her seat. This time she came flying back out the way she went in.

Then as she hit the ground she yelled, "Corky, I've got him! Get the tape."

I grabbed the enchanted tape out of my backpack and started running across the room.

"Mr. Carson, get back in your desk!"

I ignored Mr. Russell and continued toward Jill. Her arm was swinging around in a circle like she was playing with an imaginary lasso.

"Let go! Let go! Let go!" Dukey cried.

Then suddenly I could see him too.

"Pull him into your seat, Jill!"

The class could see her arm stiffen as she pulled the struggling ghost boy down. She grabbed her wrist with her other hand again and pulled harder.

"He's on the seat. Quick, tape him!"

I attached the tape to her seat back then started winding it around Dukey.

"Stop it! Stop it! Stop it!" He screamed.

"What is going on here!" Mr. Russell bellowed. "Stop this immediately and take your seats."

I kept winding the tape around and around. Higher and higher up the seat back. Around Duke's hips, then stomach, then chest. I couldn't get any around his flailing arms and kicking feet. But, when I ran out of tape he was securely fastened to the chair.

I looked at Jill and cried, "Now what?"

"Now, the flour!" She replied triumphantly.

Jill pulled the small bag of flour out of her backpack, ripped it open, then started pouring it all over Duke.

"That's enough," cried Mr. Russell, "you two will go to detention right..."

Suddenly he stopped speaking as the whole class gasped. There before them was a powdery white boy kicking and thrashing in Jill's desk.

"Oh, my gosh!" uttered Mr. Russell.

Every kid in the class jumped out of their seats. Everyone was talking at once: "Look!" "It's a kid!" "No, it's a ghost!" "Oh, My!"

Half of them rushed closer to see; the other half rushed to the other side of the room to get as far away as possible.

"Mr. Russell," Jill pointed at Duke, "this is the ghost that has been causing all the trouble for Corky. It wasn't Corky burping, or writing his name on the desk; it was him."

"I want my Mommy!"

The class gasped again. They could hear him.

"Corky and Jill are being mean to me. I want my MOMMEEE!"

He started chanting, "MOMMEEE! MOMMEEE! MOMMEEE! MOMMEEE! MOMMEEE! MOMMEEE! MOMMEEE! MOMMEEE!"

Mr. Russell walked up to Jill's desk as Duke continued his annoying chant. The whole class watched in silence as he reached around to the back of the seat and tore off a piece of the tape. He looked down at the ghost kid and ordered, "That will be enough little boy!"

Then he taped Duke's mouth shut.

The whole class started clapping.

When the applause died down, Mr. Russell said, "Young man, you are going out to the hall."

He pulled Jill's desk out of the row, then pushed it through the doorway and into the hall. When he returned, the class was buzzing with talk.

"Children, that will be enough. Take out your Social Studies book."

As I opened my book, I glanced over at Jill, who was sitting in an empty desk in the back. She gave me a thumbs up. I started to return it when I heard, "Mr. Carson, who was the 13th President of the United States?"

All right an easy one, "That was Abe... BURRRRPPP... Lincoln. Oops, excuse me."

"Another ghost, Mr. Carson?"

"Uh, no sir, that was all me!"

15 A NEW FRIEND

Several weeks passed and there was no sign of Duke. We'd finally gotten rid of him. It was nice to not constantly look over my shoulder, and not to worry about getting hit in the head with an acorn. But I was bored.

I went over to see Jill, but she was always playing dolls with her girlfriends. Ewww! Basketball season was over, and it was a few weeks before baseball season would start. Once again, I didn't have anyone to play with. So I wandered over to the park.

When I arrived, there were no kids to be seen. I walked over to the playground and sat on one of the swings. I didn't feel much like swinging so I spun around for a while. Then I just sat there and kicked the dirt with my sneaker.

I kept hoping someone would show up that I could play with. Then I realized that I was hoping to run into Duke. Seriously, I know that's nuts, but I kind of missed the little guy.

So, I started yelling his name, "DUKE... DUKE!"

"Hey Duke, are you around here Buddy?"

"Oh, Duke, come out, come out wherever you are!"

Then all of a sudden I saw his face peer shyly from behind a tree.

"Hi Duke."

"What do you want?" He asked sullenly.

"Want to play?"

"Really?" His face brightened into a smile.

"Sure. As long as you don't pelt me with acorns."

"But, you're so good at dodging them." He replied.

"How about we play hide and seek instead. But, no cheating – you can't turn invisible on me."

"OK, it's a deal. You count to ten first!"

The End

ABOUT THE AUTHOR

Robert Evans Wilson, Jr. was born in Atlanta, Georgia. He attended Georgia State University and studied philosophy, psychology, and creative writing. He is the author of *The Un-Comfort Zone*, an internationally syndicated column on motivation. He loves telling stories, and is known for making them up right on the spot. He lives in Sandy Springs, Georgia, with his two sons, both of whom are budding storytellers.